C 1995   2/96

D0470875

I

F

Tex the
Cowboy

CIP Data is available.

Published in the United States   5
by Dutton Children's Books, a division of Penguin Books USA Inc.
375 Hudson Street, New York, New York 10014
Originally published in the United Kingdom 1995
by The Bodley Head Children's Books, Random House, London.
Typography by Adrian Leichter
Printed in Singapore
First American Edition
2 4 6 8 10 9 7 5 3 1
ISBN 0-525-45418-7

TEX

the COWBOY

Sarah Garland

Dutton Children's Books

NEW YORK

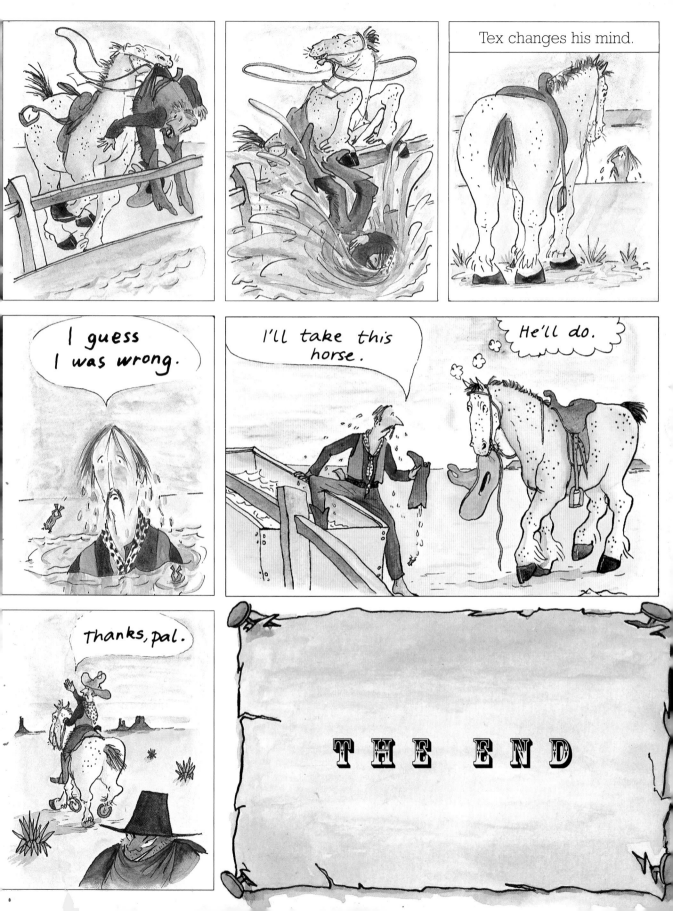

SPARKLE
GLEAM
Ladies and gentlemen, the great rodeo is about to begin.
And here is our champion rider—Hank Bones.
I AM THE GREATEST!
And our champion bull, the mighty Thunderbull.
Hank Bones has roped Thunderbull in fifty seconds.